Ma Pumpernickle's Pumpkin Patch

September

November

Pumpkin

Written by: Jeanetta DeBoef Anderson
Illustrated by: Pradip Solanki

MA PUMPERNICKLE'S PUMPKIN PATCH

Written by: Jeanetta DeBoef Anderson
Illustrated by: Pradip Solanki

Dedicated to
My special treasures:
Daniel, Cody, and Jayden Anderson

A long time ago in the town of Malow
Lived a little old lady who was a widow.

While walking one day she spotted a seed.
This was very good fortune – a treasure indeed!
For you see, our dear lady was as poor as could be
So this seed treasure made her cry out with glee!

"I shall plant this good seed and see what it brings.
Who knows if its fruit can be sold for fine things!"
She placed the seed carefully in the pocket of her skirt
Then quickly got busy digging up dirt.
She planted the seed in the well-prepared ground
Then patted and watered the little seed mound.

Day in and day out she tended it with care.
There wasn't a day that she wasn't there.
And each passing day the seed changed a bit,
'Til one day the ground started to split.
And up from that split shot a leaf bright and green.
Then another, and another could clearly be seen!

As the weeks and months passed the plant grew big and lush;
No longer a seed, but a big pumpkin bush.
And before very long to her delighted surprise
Was a beautiful pumpkin that was quite large in size!
The pumpkin was perfect, not a scratch or a nick;
It was perfectly round and quite ready to pick.

"I shall take my prize pumpkin to the fair in two days.
I'll win first place for sure," said the widow amazed.
"With the money I'll purchase a goat and a hen
Then I'll never have to go hungry again.
I shall pick it and shine it tomorrow," she said.
And with a smile on her face she scurried off to bed.

But alas, in the night snuck a hungry raccoon.
He spotted the pumpkin by the light of the moon.
And on that fateful crisp autumn night
Went up to the pumpkin and took a big bite.
So big and so round, so juicy and yummy,
The hungry raccoon filled his little coon tummy.

Early next day came the widow with glee
To polish her pumpkin, but what she did see
Made her gasp, and then cry, wring her hands in despair
For her beautiful dream had turned into a nightmare.
The pumpkin was ruined; her plans were all shattered.
Now forever she'd be hungry and her clothes would be tattered.
As she sat in despair, her head in her hands
Up walked a stranger – a kindly old man.

"Whatever is wrong that you're hopeless and blue?
Surely there's something that I can do."
Startled the widow looked up in surprise
Then shaking her head with tears in her eyes,
"Quite on the contrary kind sir," she began...
But before she could finish the kindly old man
Picked up the pumpkin and carried it away
Leaving the woman wondering in dismay!

Later he returned to knock on her door
Bringing the pumpkin he'd taken before.
But the pumpkin no longer looked ruined and dreary
It had a new look that was really quite cheery.
So amazed was the widow at this new transformation
She gazed on the stranger with true admiration!

For he had taken her hopeless despair
And given her a treasure she never knew was there.
From the pulp of the pumpkin that lay deep inside
The kindly old man made a delicious pie.
He also had harvested a large bag of seeds
That he promised when planted would meet all her needs.

Now the pumpkin never made it to the fair for first prize
But the kindly old stranger had opened her eyes.
For true treasure is found not in beauty nor size;
What lies deep within is the ultimate prize.
And from all the seeds that one pumpkin produced
Ma Pumpernickle's Pumpkin Patch was later introduced!

It was indeed the talk of the town.
People came to pick pumpkins from miles around.
And each year on her porch from September to November
Sits a neatly carved pumpkin to help her remember.

JACK O LANTERN

Little pumpkin
On the vine
You are full of
Gooey slime.

And although
You look just fine
I really want
To make you shine.

So I will polish
Inside and out
Then carve some eyes
Ears, nose and mouth.

I'll put a fire
Inside of you
So your new look
Will shine right thru.

To every passerby
You'll show
Your transformation
By your glow!

Jack o Lantern
Shining bright
Will you light
The path tonight?

Vocabulary words:

Admiration – a feeling of great respect and approval
Alas – a word used to express sadness or disappointment
Blue – sad or unhappy
Contrary – an opposite or different fact or situation
Despair – a feeling of extreme sadness or worry
Dismay – a strong feeling of being worried, disappointed, or upset
Fateful – producing a serious and usually bad result
Glee – a strong feeling of happiness
Harvested – gathered; collected
Mound – a small pile of dirt
Nick – a cut, scrape, or scratch
Produced – made or created
Purchase – to get by paying money for
Scurried – went quickly
Spotted – saw; noticed
Tattered – old and torn
Tended – took care of
Transformation – a complete or major change
Treasure – something that is very special, important, or valuable
Ultimate – the greatest
Widow – a woman whose husband has died
Wring – to twist and rub your hands together because you are nervous or upset

Discussion Questions:

What treasure did Ma Pumpernickle find?

Why was this a great treasure for her?

What did she plan to do with the pumpkin once it was grown?

What did she plan to buy with the money she made from winning the prize?

Why was she upset when she came to pick the pumpkin?

Who helped Ma Pumpernickle when she was upset about the pumpkin?

How did he help her?

What did Ma Pumpernickle learn from the kind gentleman?

Did the pumpkin make it to the fair?

What did Ma Pumpernickle do to help her remember the lesson the kind man showed her?

What lessons can you learn from this story?

Upcoming Titles by Author:

Oodles of Noodles